I0664470

1   GG Heim

G-Poems-Spot-On

by GG Heim

This work is dedicated to my ancestors who passed on the gift

of rhyming and humor about sexuality

and all future readers who support this work.

Thank you!

These poems were received by the author through

"Channeled Automatic Writing"

Thank you, Marie, for letting your space to me

Jersey City

2013

Library of Congress Cataloging-in Publication Date

Names GG Heim Author

Erotic Poetry

Subject: Poetry/Erotica/Humor

First Edition © published 2022 by GG Heim

ISBN 979-8-218-03567-9

www.g-poems-spot-on.com

All inquiries please contact: gg@g-poems-spot-on.com

Contents

Your smile

When I just see your smile
It lasts me for a while

Nourishing and sweet
I dance with light feet

When we go for a walk
I listen to your talk

Your butt I squeeze
Because I like to tease

I look into your eyes
Seeing truth, not lies

The time we spend together
Makes me feel like a feather

A fine and pleasing sight
You are just a delight

Just having you around
playing soft and sound

It lasts me for a while
When I just see your smile

Can't forget you

I can't forget you
Nor do I want to

On my skin I feel lace
craving to see your face

Allowed your wife to win
We are not of the same kin

My heart is full of pain
I refused to play your game

The choice was yours to make
Taking the real or the fake

You gave into societies rule
Can't help to think you're a fool

Still the fool is my desire
It's only you I still admire

My hope for you keeps me alive
while sipping tea around five

Now it's up to me to choose
Keep you in my memory or refuse

To you I gave my power
Fell right off the high tower

Left without any tool
Gave my all to you, you bloody fool

I imprison you into a picture frame
Refuse to be tame

Pleasure myself to the 9th degree
In my mind only you I see

All mighty God I plea
Return my power to me

Can't forget you
Nor do I want to

Brief encounter

Our encounter was so brief
But I'm shaking like a leaf

The meeting so intense
It doesn't make much sense

A stranger you are
But I know you from afar

You are my divine match
What a great catch

My blood is hot
My mind completely shot

No more with the team
Are you just a dream?

You have been so kind
Have I lost my mind?

I'm shaking like a leaf
Our encounter was so brief

I am falling for you

I am falling for you
Yes, it is true

You ignited my light
Please squeeze me tight

I'm losing all my reason
And it isn't even the season

I want you so much
Please stay in touch

I know it's not supposed to be
Because your wife can see

I feel so lost
But not at that cost

What should we do?
I know you want me too

You're rooted like a tree
And I, I fly free

Yes, it is true
I'm falling for you

The cute little hat

I like your cute little hat
With you I want to chat

Your mouth looks rather fresh
Guess with it -- you make a lot of cash

Your boobs are looking up
between them you hold a coffee cup

I love your kinky style
Adding to your sexy profile

Your legs are long and slender
My feelings strong and tender

I am a financial lender
To you my power I surrender

I know in the end I'll be broke
You causing me a deadly stroke

But it was all worth it for my cat
Who wears that cute little hat

Yearnings

My happiness you took
I'm yearning for your look

Missing your hand on my thigh
Indulging my high

My soul is far away
Searching traces of your day

Listening to my sobbing heart
Awareness that we're apart

Imagining your smiles
Wish I could stack them to piles

The sound of your voice
Did not leave me any choice

You are the most erotic
Probably I - for you the exotic

Can't breathe when I'm alone
Please rush and come home

Please give into my plea
Just come in - you have the key

The Banana

Why is the Banana crooked?
Because she grew in Phuket

What's Phuket got to do
With the Banana and you?

Because Phuket is a crooked place
And the Banana got that trace

Me, I've been visiting Phuket
And saw the Banana grow crooked

The Banana grew in Phuket
Now you know why the Banana is crooked

* Phuket is a redlight district

The Alarm

She turned on her charm
Which set off my alarm

She plays with her hair
Wiggles slightly the chair

She's pouting her lips
Obviously loving the trip

I'll lose my control
If she dances at the pole

She curves her small back
There is no lack

Her erotic demeanor
Makes me keener and keener

Now she flashes
On top of all else her lashes

In stockings she hides her legs
Wish I could rip them to rags

Observing her stare
My pants bulge-and I care

Will I be able
To get her to my stable

The urge to ride
I cannot hide

Please lady give me a break
I promise you give and take

She puts more lipstick on
Hope she's not a con

Porn plays in my head, you bet
She stands on the set

I crave to tame
This woman in her game

But her husband comes in
And keeps her from sin
So, I ---I better get a Gin

Meditation

Close your eyes and still your mind
The two halves of your brain we're trying to align

Breathe through your nose
And try to hold the pose

Straighten your back
And relax your neck

When you sing a sound
Vibration will change profound

Feel the light in your palms
It will get you to other realms

Let go of everyday life
Suspend the thrive

Repeat a mantra
While thinking of tantra

When feelings are coming
Don't stop the humming

Slowly you will enhance
Finding yourself in trance

Now you have achieved the goal
And found your soul

Hold it for an hour
You'll start to smell a flower

Now shake and awake
The Kundalini snake

It is not an easy task
To remove the mask

Repeat it again and again
One day you'll find your Zen

The light will rise
You leave behind the disguise

Feeling good is the reward
I know that strikes your chord

Meditation is the key
For real ecstasy

Obsession

You are my obsession
But I'm not your possession

Always love our session
Takes away my depression

You lose your aggression
And I come in succession

Both getting a thrill from transgression
While using a lot of discretion

In my profession
I find the greatest expression

We are getting rid of repression
Each time a great progression

Can't help my obsession
That's why I made it my profession

Horny

You are so corny
Every time you're horny

Play the romantic
Makes me rather frantic

Grabbing my behind
Certainly, well timed

Sneak around like a cat
I love it, you bet

Teasing my tush
I give you a push

Play hide and seek
You are so sleek

Especially - when I peak

Prostitution

A Prostitute takes money
That makes many feel rather funny

Some do it for free
Never charging a fee

The first has her heart intact
The second unappreciated, feels slapped

The prostitute has a bad reputation
The other one lives in her own equation

It seems like a lose - lose situation
Unless you take the married translation

All three don't have the right solution
Each has its own pollution

Stalker of my mind

You are the stalker of my mind
Really one of a kind

Whatever I think
You distract the link

Get in between the flow
Admittedly, I like it though

Tired of all this work
Craving you, my favorite perk

Reading a book
Your eyes give me a look

Trying to cook
The taste you took

In the shower
I feel your power

Your hands on my skin
Looking at your ring

Touching my breasts
Inside a pounding chest

Feel my shivering lips
From your fingertips

Your hands are sliding down
Even though you're out of town

Stroking myself for you
I wish that we were two

You were a great teacher
I crave your best feature

My legs are shaking much
Aroused I feel your touch

Circle round and round
Slowly adding sound

Wide awake instead asleep
The well is rather deep

Fingers slip inside
Back and forth delight

You're at my side
Working up a tide

Breathing fast
Make it last

Only for you my treasure
I burst now with pleasure

The sock

Don't put your cock
In a restraining sock

I hate that so much
Not enough touch

Keep it natural man
You don't like to eat out of a can

Get rid of the sock
quick show me that cock

No need for a lock
Just gently knock

I lick you with my tongue
Huge you will become

Drive on course
I will guide you to source

Strike you with light
It's good so tight

Reach high
Yeah, that's my guy

Very gently I slide
Stay strong, don't hide

Eat my inner thigh
Oh, I almost die

You know that's all I wanted
My mind is oh so haunted

You are my obsession
Finally understanding my lesson

So hot indulged in sweat
work and wait until I'm wet

Dissolve me into a lake
Now - have your cake

Enter me - not rough
But be just a little tough

Back off a bit
Play my tit

Keep going my hunk
In trance I sunk

Please keep me there
That's true care

Close your eyes, be blind
Read my mind

Love my brain
Keep me sane

Don't be lame
I take all the blame

Cut off this cock
I want to keep him in my dock

I want to keep and not give back
Unbearable the lack!

Come on let's hit the sack
Once more on my back

Finger me up--- up ---up
Preferably in the tub

Give me a cuddle
Please produce a bubble

I tingle all over
You are such a rover

You are my King
For you I will sing

Spare the bling
Don't need a ring

But treat me with respect
That means no neglect

Want all your attention
It adds another dimension

Give me all your time
Not just an hour at nine

Make me number one
That will make me come

In bed I will hum
That's the whole lump sum

Spare the sock
Just give me that cock

The Mirror

In front of the mirror, I stand
Watching my own hands

They want to explore
Now I'm afraid that I'm a whore

Pleasure is screaming for release
She knows very well how to tease

The old brainwashing is in the way
In the matter – do I have a say

How can I free my soul?
Can you help me, make me whole?

Just forget about the old stuff
Even though it's tough

Starting with your eyes
Make up will advise

Some color for the lip
and all is hip

The hair you just brush
No need for hush hush

It's ok to do all that
You want to get laid - flat

Arrange those boobies tight
In a lacy bra, that's right

Now place your little butt
In a tiny thong - "but " - shut up

Put on your high heeled shoes
and drink a little bit of booze

Play the music, not too loud
You have all reason to be proud

Light a candle in the room
That'll make everything bloom

Then go to the loo
Spritz a little fragrance too

Now imagine this good-looking hunk
To the bottom of your bosom, he sunk

He's drunk with your charm
Won't do you any harm

Light a fire
Grant him his desire

Take off his cap
And sit on his lap

Circle your hips in large loops
You can be sure nothing droops

Once he's large and full of greed
Whisper in his ear a little tweet

When he's really ready,
Take it slow and steady

Withdraw here and there
Deny him his share

Make him beg you much
Just for a tiny little touch

Kiss him on the back
What the heck

Use your pussy wise
Let him rise and rise and rise

Grab him soft and hard
He'll stand straight "en garde"

Allow him entrance slow
That will make him glow

Ride the wild horse
But stay on course

Give him your all
He will always call

While down on his knees
Not yet aware of the fees

Never mind the scam
He loves to pay for the ham

Girl it is all right
Just squeeze him tight

Rock his boat a bit
With just one Tit

Play also a little game
Not always the same

Involve his brain
It'll get him on the train

Open the tunnel
You don't need a funnel

He'll find his way
Then you have the say

Be happy little chick
Being his whore is a good trick

It's the way to his heart
While he thinks he's super smart

No need for the old stuff
The church is just a bluff

Enjoy Sex
Remember, just not with your EX

Gentleman

Into your eyes I gaze
Surroundings are a haze

Reality's a blur
You're calling me Sir

Seems I've known you forever
Your touch is very clever

I accepted your play
Yet you keep me at bay

You offered me your body
Still somehow, I feel shoddy

Trying to find the connection
Breaking your protection

You are shivering and trembling
It feels like you I'm disassembling

What's the matter my girl
Please tell me, I love your curl

Sir, I am a virgin
But the money is for a surgeon

My mother is rather ill
Has already a broken will

Please be careful with me
I am about to flee

Please help me help my mother
I hope nobody will discover

The deed I'm about to do
Keep the secret, would you?

My child, I want you to get dressed
Calm down no reason for stress

Here is the money for your mother
About all else don't even bother

I admire your courage
And propose to you for marriage

Your heart is on the right spot
To me that means a lot

Operating Manual

(How to handle a woman)

Tonight, you begin
By touching her skin

Kiss her neck
Then stroke the back

Gaze into her eyes
Don't tell her lies

Whisper into her ears
Wipe away the tears

Wiggle those boobies
Give her a necklace of rubies

Hold her around the waist
You have such good taste

Caress her behind
You are so very kind

Admire her legs
For more she begs

Tickle her toes
You won't be foes

Believe my adage
Her feet you should massage

Now get on with her thighs
That will bring on highs

Gently now push
Her little tush

Slightly open her lips
With your fingertips

Play to get her flow
Line up right and row

Try to enhance
Step inside and dance

Hold your desire
She needs more fire

Make her mad
She'll be so glad

Give her just a bit
Enough to tease her clit

She sure will weep
If you now go to sleep

The way things are

It's easier I find
When you do the thinking
And I relax my mind

I am using my guts
But you don't understand
And tell me to shut up

Holding me in cuffs
When you do the talking
That, for me --- is tough

It's not very polite
When you interrupt
While I recite

I use my intuition
You take apart the whole ignition
I'm already on to a new mission

It's better when I drive
You refuse to ask for direction
When I already have arrived

When I am right
Your ego puts up a huge fight
That's just the way things are - good night

I hope the next generation
For woman's elation

Will find a solution
For man's evolution

Hopeless case

Yes, Sir
You can have her

Just make sure
That you have the cure

She's rather ill
I can't pay that bill

She does not want to drink
Perhaps you can find the link

She does not want food
Maybe she takes your loot

Please take her away
I guess she likes your sway

I have had enough
Could be I was too tough

Goodbye my dear
I'll stay here

We have to part
He has the better card

I'll always remember you
And miss your tiny shoe

Goodbye my little dove
I send you with love

I wish I would have known before
That I can't treat you like a whore

I was a fool
You are not a tool

The fault is all mine
Hope he gives you a better time

You can have her,
Yes, Sir

Obsolete

Men are obsolete
Did you already get that tweet?

Women just love guys too much
Crave to be close to their touch

We could impregnate ourselves
And put them on a shelf

We could freeze their semen
Free ourselves of the demon

They are living on sheer grace
But it would be boring without the chase

Guys once this fact gets out
You better behave and watch out

Some women might use this news
And finally get rid of their blues

We really want you in bed
As an antidote to sad

If you are not a fool
You might be an exception to the rule

All others need to bring out a new edition
Preferable with a bit more submission

Get rid of the violent streak
That'll make us women peak

You better lay at women's feet
Be aware that you are obsolete

MAN, you frighten me so much
Abuse your might and touch

Beat the crap out of me
For nothing don't you see

Your anger's target I am
Taking the hit for Uncle Sam

Your only safe shelter is woman's womb
In exchange you put her in a tomb

A woman is NOT to be treated like that

CHANGE YOUR MIND
Cuddle with her instead

Beware! She's just a loan
Make her laugh and moan
She's always her own

Be gentle and soft
Sleep with her in the loft

Kiss her lips and face
Keep an even pace

Run your fingers through her hair
Caress her shapely pair

Tickle her slightly
Squeeze her tightly

Slide your tongue below her waist
You will surely hit her taste

Explore her inner thigh
Be careful she might cry

Not because she's shy
Rather bad memories to defy

Once you conquered the hill
Be quiet....... be still

Look at the delight
So gorgeous, so bright

Patiently kindle the snake
Now she's yours to take

Shiny and moist
Willingly your hoist

Slowly, slowly, slowly
Don't destroy the holy

Get swallowed in the fire
Enjoy your greatest desire

Push her firmly high
Listen to her sigh

Delight in her raging rose
Time to try another pose

Add your phantasy
And fuel much ecstasy

Possess and fulfill the cave
Steadily surfing her wave

For hours and hours and hours
Indulge now in your well-deserved powers

Dick

It's all about your dick
Sometimes it almost makes me sick

Your dick is in my thought
In this prison I am caught

Your dick is on my mind
Sometimes in my clit I find

Your dick is big and large
For me without a charge

I have no need for tee
Your dick is satisfying me

Your dick is a teaser
That makes you a pleaser

Your dick is fantastic
So very elastic

Your dick is dripping
Me enjoying the sipping

Your dick is rather fat
You are such a rat

Your dick is pleasing me
Luckily for free

Your dick is all you had
Be happy, be glad

Your dick is the best
Your dick passed my test

Your dick is teasing my eye
So don't be shy

Your dick is sometimes tired
No reason to get fired

Your dick is standing straight
Looking for the gate

Your dick is easy to handle
Smooth and hot like a candle

Your dick is my all
Hope you stand tall

Your dick is your potential
I'm approving this credential

Your dick is in my head
So don't be sad

I promise, like a tick
I'll hang on to your DICK

The Tiny Little Clit

I love my tiny little clit
And she -- she loves to spit

She's a bit demanding
Careful with the landing

My clit is flying high
Just not when you leave her dry

So please work a bit
On my little clit

Love her skin
Pleasure she will bring

I can tell
If you behave well

I'll allow you to sit
On my little clit

Be a good lover
That's your cover

Enjoy the clit
And kiss her tit

Get her to dance
Use your lance

An explosion will be lit
When you kiss that clit

Love her, love it
Love the tiny little clit

Make her gorgeous and keen
Then she's your melting queen

Look at the outer and inner
Never mind you're not a sinner

See my clit swell
You do that so well

That's the goal
That will please her soul

Eat my tit
Love my clit

Get drunk a bit
Then she will spit

My tiny little Clit

About the Author

GG Heim enthusiastically received "G-Poems-Spot-On" through automatic writing

Previously GG practiced healing arts through
Quantum Biofeedback with William Nelson (NASA / Desiree Dubounet).

From 1997 until 2009 she thrived as a Licensed
NYC Real Estate Broker located in the Empire State Building.

In her younger years the author managed 50 Salespeople for Tupperware.

GG is a Graduate of several workshops such as Vipassana / Goenka

Guided for 20 years by a beloved Spiritual Master named Rev. Dr. Hedy Milicevic,
2016/17 she lived and studied several months in an Ashram in India with
His Divine Holiness the Pontiff of Hinduism Bhagavan Sri Nithyananda Paramashivam.
She still is dedicated and devoted to "Swamiji" in gratitude, love and admiration.

GG lived and worked 1.5 years in Hawaii with lovely Japanese Master Akiko Masuda.

She is expressly voicing her gratitude and love to her daughter, teachers and Guru.

GG Heim is a Yogi, "Jeevan Mukti" and Self Realized Master

She has traveled numerous countries and continents, loves to read, write and dance.

GG Heim was born in Southern Germany and immigrated to New York City at age 35.

She lives a nomadic lifestyle and frequently changes her address.

GG is a mother of two and grandmother of four: I LOVE YOU ALL

GG@g-poems-spot-on.com

www.G-Poems-Spot-on.com

www.ingramcontent.com/pod-product-compliance
Lightning Source LLC
Chambersburg PA
CBHW08083250626
47160CB00008B/2949